DATE DUE			

31280111052200
Donohue, Moira Rose.

E
DON

Penny and the
Punctuation Bee

Penny and the Punctuation Bee

Moira Rose Donohue

Illustrated by Jenny Law

Albert Whitman & Company, Morton Grove, Illinois

In memory of my parents, Doris and Joe.—M.R.D.

For Etienne, my little ray of sunshine.—J.L.

Library of Congress Cataloging-in-Publication Data

Donohue, Moira Rose.
Penny and the Punctuation Bee / by Moira Rose Donohue ; illustrated by Jenny Law.
p. cm.
Summary: When Penny, a period, competes in her school's annual punctuation bee, she is especially
determined to beat Elsie, an exclamation point who is loud and boastful.
ISBN 978-0-8075-6477-6 (hardcover)
[Period (Punctuation)—Fiction. English language—Punctuation—Fiction.]
I. Law, Jenny, 1975- ill. II. Title.
PZ7.D7223325 Pen 2008 [E]—dc22 2007030957

The design is by Carol Gildar.

For more information about Albert Whitman & Company,
please visit our web site at www.albertwhitman.com.

MR. DASH
READING TEACHER

PUNCTUATION BEE
FRIDAY 2:00

Penny stopped short when she saw the sign on Mr. Dash's door.

Penny, a period, was good at stopping. That's why she was on the safety patrol.

SAFETY PATROL

The hallway was crowded with punctuation marks. Connie, a comma, and Penny's best friend, Quentin, a question mark, joined her to read the sign: "Punctuation Bee Friday, 2:00."

READ-A-THON

PUNCTUATION BEE
FRIDAY 2:00

SAFETY PATROL

"Are you signing up? Should I?" asked Quentin.

"Save the questions for your next school newspaper article and just do it," said Penny.

Quentin pulled a pencil from the spiral binding on his reporter's note pad. He wrote his name and handed the pencil to Penny.

Elsie, an exclamation point, bounced up in her cheerleader uniform.

"Yay! The Punctuation Bee! An exclamation point has won for the last three years!" she said.

"Maybe it's time someone else won," said Penny.

Elsie looked at the sign-up list. "Not likely, if *this* is the competition!"

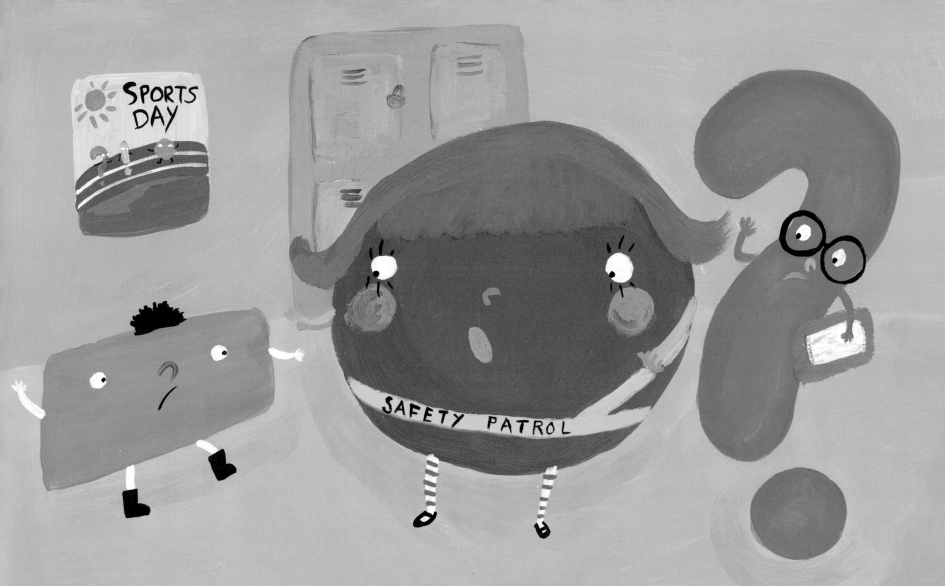

Penny turned to Quentin. "Exclamation points are *so* loud. Let's go practice."

"Where? When? Should we get a snack?"

"Quentin, stop the questions. We have work to do."

As they walked away, a hyphen dashed by. "Stop running," said Penny, in her best patrol voice.

WIN

READ

BOOK

PAD

STOP

SAFETY PATROL

At Penny's house, the two friends wrote words on note cards.

Quentin held up "WIN" and turned over the thirty-second timer. Penny had
to make a sentence using the word and her punctuation mark.

Penny stared at the word and thought hard. Then she said, "We won't let Elsie win."

"We won't?" Quentin asked.

Penny shook her head firmly. "No, we won't."

Then Penny held up "CAT."

"The cat chased the dog," said Quentin.

Penny laughed. "That's funny, but it's not a question."

Quentin tried again. "Did you ever see a cat chase a dog?"

"Good job," said Penny.

They practiced for two hours. Finally, Quentin held up the word "PIE."

"I love apple pie!" said Penny.

"No, that's an exclamation. Are you tired? Do you want to stop?"

Before Penny could answer, her mother announced that Quentin's dad was there to pick him up.

My cat's name is Dottie.

After dinner, Penny went to her room to practice by herself. She made declarative sentences about everything there. "The picture is crooked. My cat's name is Dottie."

"Penny, you should get some sleep," said her dad as he handed her hot cocoa and tucked her in.

"I have to practice if I want to beat Elsie," said Penny, taking a sip.

"The cocoa is hot. My pillow is . . . " She fell asleep in the middle of a sentence.

The picture is crooked.

The cocoa is hot.

The next day, at 2:00 on the dot, the contestants lined up outside the gym.
Connie was first, followed by Collin, a colon; Stella, an asterisk; Penny; and Quentin.
The quotation mark twins, Quinn and Lynn, rolled up, chattering breathlessly.
Penny felt fizzy, like a shaken-up soda. Quentin tapped her on the shoulder.

SAFETY PATROL

"Are you nervous? Are you ready?" he asked.

"I think I'm ready," Penny said. "Good luck!"

They filed into the gym. The entire school was squished
together on the floor. Penny's mother waved from the audience.
"Contestants, please sit down," said Mr. Dash.
Penny noticed an empty chair. Where was Elsie?

"Sorry I'm late!" said Elsie, hopping through the gym. "I just made cheerleading captain! Yay!"
Bragger, thought Penny.

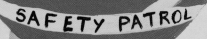

"Take your seat, Elsie," said Mr. Dash.

"Contestants, when I call your name, please approach the microphone. Phrase your answer in the form of a sentence, and use your punctuation mark correctly." He pointed to the shiny trophy. "The winner will receive this prize. Good luck, everyone."

The first contestant was Connie the comma.

Mr. Dash held up the word "PEAS."

Connie smiled. "My brother hates carrots, beans, and especially peas."

The school secretary typed the sentence. It appeared on a big screen.

"Well done," said Mr. Dash. "One point for—wait! That sentence has two commas. Let me check the official Punctuation Bee rules. Yes, Connie earns an extra point for using two commas."

The scoreboard pinged, and the number "2" lit up next to Connie's name.

My brother hates carrots, beans, and especially peas.

Then Quentin's turn came. Mr. Dash held up "PIRATES."

"Do pirates wear pajamas?" asked Quentin.

Everyone laughed. The other newspaper reporters whooped and whistled as the scoreboard lit up a "1" for Quentin.

Elsie just rolled her eyes.

That made Penny more determined than ever to win.

Penny was next. She got the word "STREET."
She tugged nervously on her safety patrol belt. A thought flashed through her mind.
"Always wait behind the safety patrol before crossing the street."
The safety patrol squad applauded, and "1" lit up next to Penny's name.

Elsie jumped up to the microphone before her name was even called.

Mr. Dash held up the word "FLIP."

"I can do a flip!" she shouted.

And she did one.

The cheerleaders in the audience did flips, too.
Show-offs, thought Penny.

The bee continued. One by one, punctuation marks dropped out. Even Connie finally ran out of things to list.

"We're down to the final three contestants—Quentin, Penny, and Elsie," said Mr. Dash. "We'll continue until only one mark is left—but now you will each get the same word. I'll ask Penny and Elsie to turn around and cover their ears until called."

Quentin approached the microphone. Mr. Dash held up "TEACHER."

"Who is your teacher?" said Quentin.

"Very good," said Mr. Dash. "This time, Elsie is next."

Elsie turned around. "My teacher is terrific!"

Mr. Dash called Penny.

She turned and looked at the word. She tapped her chin. Nothing came.

"Five seconds," said Mr. Dash.

Penny looked at him and blurted out, "Mr. Dash is my teacher."

Ping. She got another point.

Mr. Dash is my teacher.

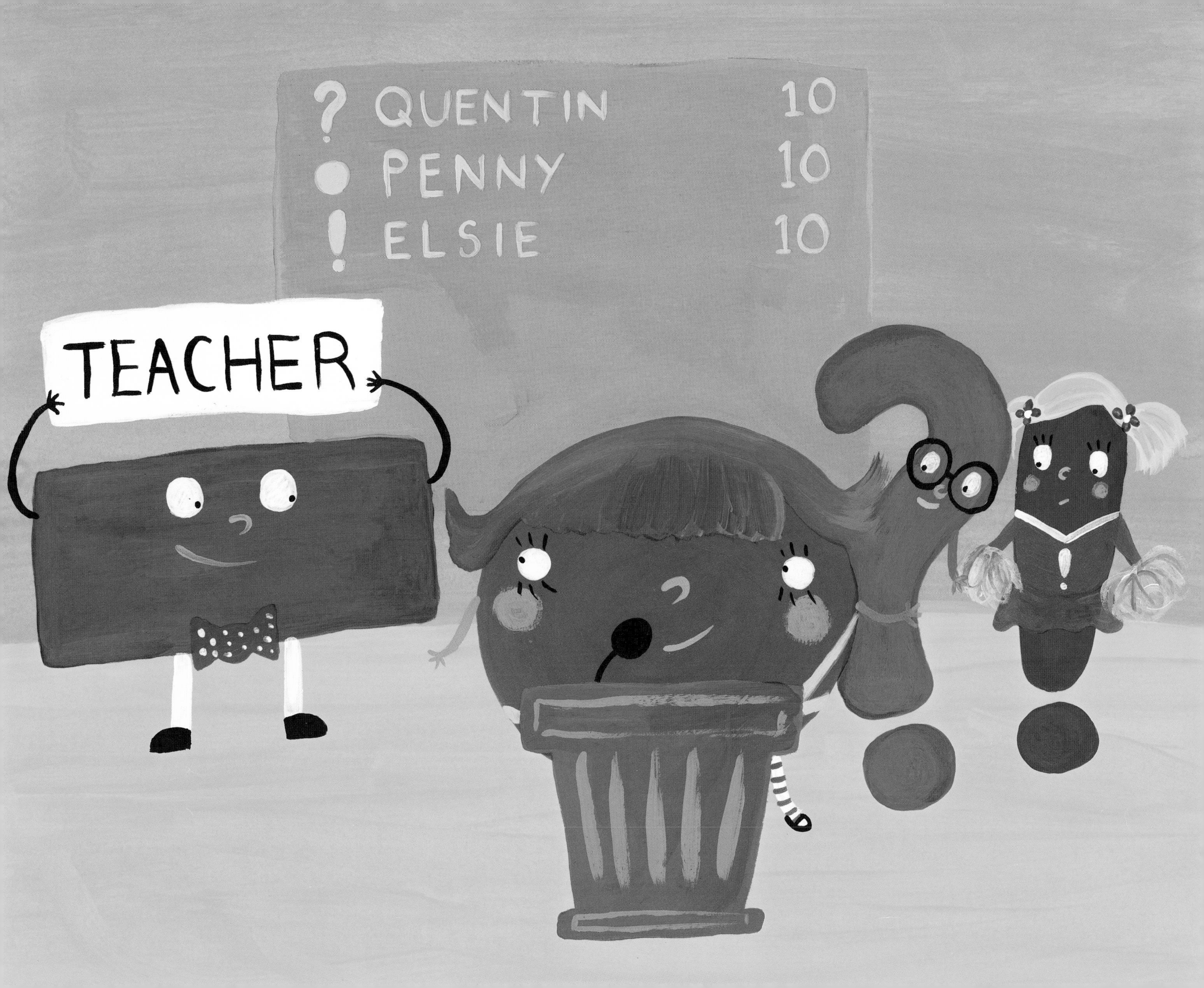
? QUENTIN 10
PENNY 10
! ELSIE 10
TEACHER

Suddenly the loudspeaker hummed to life.

"Students, the buses are here. Please return to your classrooms for dismissal," boomed the voice of the principal.

"Well, it appears we have a three-way tie," said Mr. Dash.

A tie? They hadn't beaten Elsie! Penny looked at Quentin. He was pointing to the screen.

"Mr. Dash? What about Penny's abbreviation?" asked Quentin.

"That's right," said Penny. Her class had just learned to make abbreviations. "I used a period twice—once after 'Mr.' and once at the end of the sentence."

She held her breath.

? QUENTIN   ★ 10 ★
● PENNY   ★ 1*1 ★
! ELSIE   10

"Penny and Quentin are right—Penny gets
an extra point!" said Mr. Dash.
The scoreboard whistled and pinged and
flashed like fireworks on the Fourth of July.

"Congratulations to our champion!" Mr. Dash handed
Penny the sparkling trophy.
The crowd cheered.
Elsie drooped until she looked like a question mark.

? QUENTIN   10
● PENNY   11
! ELSIE   10

Penny held out the trophy to Quentin. And although it meant using an exclamation point, she said,

"Quentin, we did it!"

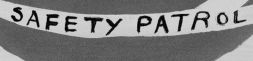

About the Period

All sentences end in one of three punctuation marks. The declarative sentence ends with a period. Can you guess that an interrogative sentence (also known as a question) ends with a question mark? Use an exclamation point for some commands (imperative sentences), like "Stop fighting!" And I'm sure you know how to use one for an exclamation!

Of the three final punctuation marks, only the period has another job. A period after a word in a sentence tells the reader that the word has been shortened, or abbreviated. For example, "Mr." is the abbreviation for "Mister," and "U.S." is the abbreviation for "United States."

The punctuation bee is the author's invention. But you might want to try one in your own classroom!